THE PHANTOM'S TEA

ALL ARE WELCOME AT THE SILENT CIRCUS

...BUT HOW DO I GET OUT OF HERE?

DANICA MENDEZ-LIAKOS

ISBN: 978-1-7347852-0-3

Whilst every effort has been made to ensure that the information
contained within this book is correct at the time of going to press,
the author and publisher can take no responsibility for the errors or
omissions contained within.

Book design by Wordzworth
www.wordzworth.com

For Daddy & Little Lou
Thank you to my best friend
and husband Matthew

THE PHANTOM'S TEA

There's a place in the darkness
It shouldn't involve me
But I know if you go there
You'll hear the Phantom's Tea.

With every sip the Phantom takes
He gives you quite a tale
Alone and scared you'll soon become
This happens without fail.

So listen at your own risk
Be careful what you do
Join his table if you dare
But the tea will soon star you.

CONTENTS

CHAPTER ONE

Be

I drowned. The quicksand filled my ears and built heavy brick walls inside them, leaving me trapped in my own mind forever. My body was stuck, that was for sure. But now my thoughts were cornered between my ears with no way of escaping, thanks to the quicksand! I knew that every single grain of terror was working its way to my brain. Each breath I took filled my lungs with its toxic pieces that felt like tiny needles filling my chest. I would never know what fresh air was like again. My eyes then turned to stone and time became frozen. The only friend I had left was my own heartbeat, which was drumming a lively song through the rushing of the sand!

This is the fate I had never imagined for myself. But you're about to get the real story. I almost wish the chilly clutches of the sand invited me all the way down. That would be less complicated than what I have to live with now.

I was in so deep, my body felt like heavy steel. The deeper I sank, the colder I felt as my chills helped the sand gain a firmer grip to drag me down to the unknown. Was I becoming ice…or stone? "Help!" I yelled. Who am I kidding? My voice ran from me long ago. The hair-raising grip of the quicksand had me at its mercy. I accepted my fate:

no one would ever find or know what happened to me. For some reason, I felt like there was another world just beyond the quicksand and something—or someone—got me right where they wanted!

I remember reading once that in order to escape quicksand you need to slowly pull your body out like you're in slow motion. So, I began to gently hoist my heavy body upwards. As I lifted my arms, I saw the murky, sticky sand drip down. Gross! There was something really vile about this quicksand! In fact, it was almost like a green, hairy paste!

I escaped the grips of death by grabbing onto solid ground and worming my way to safety. As I lay there, I tried to catch my breath but it was clearly running for its own life! My heart was bursting. *Thump! Thump!* "Maybe the worst is over? I managed to whisper to myself. Nope, not even close. Time stood still for a moment. As I looked up into the black abyss of a sky, I saw something peculiar.

Is that a window? I wondered. *A window in the sky? No! That is not a sky! What is it?* The sand in my eyes complicated things a bit. Suddenly, I felt this overwhelming itchy feeling on my feet and legs. It felt as if a slew of microscopic electric eels were biting at my toes! I shot up and looked down. What I saw almost made me want to dive back into the sand!

So, as it turns out, that wasn't sand I was drowning in. Not at all! It was trillions of tiny, green radioactive spiders! They were glowing, quick moving, and if you looked closely they were see-through! You could even see their tiny blue brains!

Thrashing around like I was suddenly taken by a tornado, I began to shed some of the spiders. *This is impossible*, I thought! My hectic dance of panic came to a sudden stop because of a shrilling sound from above. *CRASH!* I squinted my eyes toward the sky where I saw what looked to be a bunch of words etched into a black void. Since when does the sky talk? The sky twitched with color like scrambled reception on a TV screen. Finally, I could read the words:

Here's to hoping we get some rain!
Wash away the spiders
before they get to your brain!

That was all the confirmation I needed! I continued to twist and turn to escape the grip of the little green fiends. They were small, but boy were they mighty! Every time one would drop to the ground I would pulverize it until it became nothing but green dust! I let out a sigh of relief and made a mad dash for what looked like an exit. "I'm getting out of here," I chanted to myself as I ran for my life. That's when things went black.

I woke up to an incredibly eerie combination of sounds and took my first breath. It was the thickest air I had ever breathed. I decided to take it slow. If I took more shallow breaths, maybe I wouldn't take in so much of the dust. The sound of my own heartbeat sang along to the tunes of creepy circus music which sounded like it was playing from an old record player dying a slow, miserable death! Suddenly it all made sense. I was in a circus? As the circus music continued to roar, the wild horses inside my chest began to break free. My heartbeat became louder than anything in the room. Then came the goosebumps. I will never forget the unfriendly clutch of those shivers that invaded my entire body! They were so strong

I had to check if my goosebumps were actually spiders.

Most of all, I'll never forget the moment I became both ringleader and side show act of The Worst Show on Earth. Let me be clear, I *did* choose my own destiny—I just wish someone would have told me to be careful when choosing which door to walk through. Door number one? Door number two? Door number three? I guess none of it matters now! Does it?

CHAPTER TWO

Careful

Today is July 27th...I think. It has officially been one year since I woke up here without a clue. My name is Hal, and if you close this book, I will forever be lost in its pages. I do exist! I am a real person! More than anything, I need your help.

Imagine waking up on the floor in the middle of a circus ring. That's what happened to me. I don't know how I got there;

all I know is when I opened my eyes, the life I once lived was gone without a trace. The silence of my very existence was so loud. I guess it's possible to be in such a quiet place that your own ears will trick you into thinking you're smothered in sirens. I was at the circus, there was no doubt. But I was also the last boy on earth.

Don't close the book yet! Let me explain a few things first. Maybe I can save you from ending up here, too!

CHAPTER THREE

Which

I remember that summer very well. It was on fire! Each day was long, sticky, and hot. In the afternoons, it was hard to take a deep breath without suffocating in heat. The stagnant clasp of the sun's heat would invade your nostrils and lungs like menacing, green spiders of doom! After a long school year, all any kid wants to do is relax by the lake and maybe take a long hike down the shoreline.

However, my parents always had different plans for me!

Every summer, my parents would insist I go to my grandparents' house in Horrington Springs, or as I like to call it, Horror Springs. Everyone and everything seems to move at a snail's pace in Horror Springs, and it's certainly no place for a kid who loves a good adventure! Imagine spending your summer days and nights with stuffy old people who like to just sit in the air conditioning and talk about the "good ole days?" My "good ole days" have just begun, and I wasn't going to get to them faster hanging out in Horror Springs! My parents would always say, "We want you to find happiness with the simple things in life, Hal!"

Simple things? HA! I laugh in the face of simple things! Why should you be satisfied with a simple flame when you can have any of the brilliant beams of light that surround you? Am I right? Well…maybe if I were you, I wouldn't take advice from someone like me. I'm not exactly in the best position right now.

My mom and dad also sent me to Horror Springs because every school year, I somehow managed to get myself into a good deal of trouble. I'll admit it; I was a bit of a trouble-maker at school! I've also been known to be quite a prankster! I used to be proud of that title, but now I'm ashamed. Power and popularity do not come from putting others down. I was wrong about that.

Since Horror Springs is nothing but a gigantic snooze-fest, naturally I brought some of my pranks along with me to spice things up a bit! I wanted to paint the boring black and white walls of this place with the colors of mischief and laughter. I could fill librar-ies with stories of the pranks I've pulled on the poor residents of Horror Springs! Just thinking about them cracks me up! Man, those were the days! But things are very different now. In fact, the only story I should be focused on right now is the one you need to know in order to set me free!

It was the last day of school, which meant the second the bell rang, I was whisked into a car to drive all the way up to Horror Springs. Usually, my parents play boring music the entire way, but something was different about this time. My parents didn't play music; they didn't even speak much during the three-hour trip. I didn't say much either. There was something strange about this ride to Horror Springs; to this day I can't put my finger on it. Everything just seemed like a weird blur.

I'd like to tell you that the ride to Horror Springs is miserably boring, but it really isn't. At certain points, the trip can be quite beautiful. We would always pass this waterfall called

Burrsir Falls, which is remarkable! Close your eyes and imagine the bluest blue you've ever seen. Now imagine if there were flashes of pure white light that sparkle through the sapphire water falling from the top of a cliff down to a glistening lake like shooting stars in the daylight. The twinkling reflection of the sky and clouds would fill the water with such beauty! Passing Burrsir Falls was always the best part of going to Horror Springs. But this time, Burrsir Falls—and everything for that matter—looked very foreign.

I felt every single bump on the road. A little pebble felt like it could send the car careening into a ditch. Every scent that filled the air, whether it was freshly cut grass or the smell of a truck's gasoline, led me into a spiral of nausea and misery. "Yikes," I complained to my parents! "What could possibly be in the air this year?" The most unsettling part of the whole trip was the scenery. Listen, I hated going to Horror Springs, but at least I had pretty stuff to look at on the way up! This year, on the other hand, was abysmal. My eyes searched desperately for some splashes of color. Where is that blue sky? How about the deep green trees and the brilliantly yellow flowers that looked like sunbeams floating on the rolling hills of the springs? Where was any sign of life? Everything just looked so…BLAH!

The outskirts of Horror Springs were engulfed in a dreary haze that trapped any kind of color from standing out. The sky was icy gray like a winter storm was about to whip through! The trees were a deep brown like they were bracing themselves for the first fall chill to come and steal all of their leaves. The lakes and rivers appeared to have a tint of grayish-green as if they were copying the bad mood of the sky. Worst of all, Burrsir Falls was swallowed in a fog patch. Out of all my years passing through Burrsir Falls, I had never seen haze before. The entire surroundings of Burrsir Falls were nothing but a thick smog of wretched mystery. It was like something…or someone…was trying to warn me.

Finally, we arrived in my grandparents' neighborhood. Goodbye, summer! As we pulled up to the house, I saw a group of about seven kids playing basketball down the road. They seemed different…like they were shadows dancing cryptically through the fog. Emotionless. Usually when you play a game, there are a ton of different faces you make! These kids had one empty, blank stare the entire time I was watching. Even the colors of their clothing were so bland and washed out. Not one kid stood out; it was like they all blended into one identity. Had I just seen the living dead? How could a bunch of kids play basketball and not have any expression on their faces? How could they be so slow moving, too? The lights were on behind their eyes, but it was clear that nobody was home. Were they even human? Probably—even aliens wouldn't be seen acting that boring! Dull! Dull! Dull! Bland! Bland! Bland! This was going to be a very long summer.

I hopped out of the car to help my dad unload the truck when my comic book collection went crashing to the pavement and sent a slight rumble beneath my feet. Since when did my collection weigh one-thousand pounds? All the freaky neighborhood kids stopped playing ball dead in their tracks and turned to face me…all at the same time. They were in perfect unison. Having seven sets of those creepy eyes on me immediately caused the hair on the back of my neck to rise with fear and curiosity. I felt like my own instinct was warning me that something bad was about to happen. "Hey! You weirdos! What are you looking at?" I barked at the kids. It was as if my yelling meant nothing. Did they even hear me? I screamed louder. "Why don't you just mind your own business, FREAKS?!"

Suddenly their eyes widened and their gaze locked onto me. It was as if their eyes turned into two giant oceans of dark mystery! I felt like if I moved an inch closer I could fall into their bottomless eyes and drown. They continued to stare at me like I was some clown at the…circus. I knelt down to pick up my collection when I saw a comic book I didn't recognize. As I picked it up to get a closer look, I immediately dropped it and shrieked in pain! I don't know what it was, but the comic book felt like it was negative five-hundred degrees! If you've ever touched hot ice before, that is how it felt! In one way it was one-million degrees, in another way it felt like I was doing a handstand without gloves on an iceberg! The comic book fell to the ground when I suddenly saw the darkness of a shadow consume the cover. One of the creepy neighborhood kids snatched the comic from the ground with one hand and immediately grabbed my hand with another. I shuddered as I felt his cold hand touch mine. I thought at any moment I could turn into ice.

"Hey man, what's your problem," I yelled?

"Sorry, I was just trying to help," he whispered.

There was something about his eyes. He reminded me of how pathetic Burrsir Falls looked while we were driving to Horror Springs. I decided to be nice to the kid, something I find difficult to do.

"Sorry," I said. "I just want to go back home."

The boy looked at me as if he had every answer to any questions anyone could ever ask about me. In a defeated mutter, the kid took a few steps closer and asked where I was from.

"What business is it of yours?" I bit back. *All of these weird, nosy freaks at Horror Springs better watch out*, I thought to myself. *I have a mouth and I am not afraid to use it.*

"Sorry for asking. My name is Wilde. Have you ever read that comic book before?" he asked, pointing at the icy comic book.

"Yes, I have," I lied. "Now if you'll excuse me."

Wilde stood up and pointed at me as if he was pointing a dagger straight at my heart. He jumped up like he was being electrocuted and hysterically screamed, "Liar! You haven't even opened it at all! You—". Wilde was blaring, but his face did not change. It was like something was holding him back from showing any emotion! He kept looking over his shoulder, too. Like he was scared someone was watching. Who was he so afraid of? I stopped him right there with a swift kick to the back of his knees. Man, did that kid go down!

"Stay out of my face, Wilde," I warned, "Or trouble will find you!"

He looked at me and said, "Trouble has already found you." What a freak! Trouble is no match for me!

I walked inside my grandparents' house with all of my comic books. I didn't even turn back, yet I could *feel* Wilde still watching me. It was as if he knew everything about me. The stare of his eyes felt like they were burning a hole in my back. His creepy linger made its way deep within my soul. Suddenly I was being eaten alive by chills! The chills were like Wilde's weird little grip gaining control of me.

"Oh well," I said, trying to shrug it off, "he will be the one I pull my first prank on."

Standing here today I could tell you this; I wish I never pulled my first prank on Wilde. I wish I was nicer! In some ways I wish I never met him! What is even crazier? I would do anything in the world if he could be my friend! I also wish I opened that comic book the second my foot hit the ground of Horror Springs. Maybe things would be different?

CHAPTER FOUR

Door

The shrieks of the summer crickets pierced my ears like the echo of whining bells. It was a hot sticky summer that made even the toughest kids uncomfortable. I was replaying the conversation with Wilde in my mind over and over like I was trapped in some sort of weird movie theater inside my own brain! Why was he so interested in that comic book? I decided to do some investigating and made my way upstairs to the bedroom I was staying in. My comic book collection was on the top shelf of the closet. I decided to grab a small ladder and take the box down so I can get a closer look at the weird mystery comic. I carried the heavy box down and set it on my windowsill. There was no way I was going to grab it without some protection, so I found an old ripped pair of gloves at the bottom of an empty drawer and put them on.

As I sifted through the collection, a firefly slipped into my room through the open window in front of me. The firefly quickly flew one lap around the room then hovered over my comic book collection. His little light was shining in unison with the powerful beam of the moon! I was hypnotized by its magic! He looked like a little firework! My eyes locked onto the light of the bug and

I began to swoon back and forth. Back and forth. Back and forth. Back and forth.

Suddenly, the firefly's light stopped as he dropped right into my box. It was like his wings and light was turned off by some merciless switch! My eyes followed the fly as he lay on top of the mystery comic, his light flickering with weakness. I think he was trying to tell me something. I gently lifted the bug out of the box and onto my windowsill. The firefly spread his wings, ignited a shine, and flew straight toward the moon like he was a tiny lightning bolt of fury. "Well," I said, "at least someone is getting out of Horror Springs." I adjusted my gloves and picked up the creepy comic.

The cover was quite ominous. An old tattered circus tent stood strong against the powerful strikes of cold rain. The night was pure black with no moon to help guide the way for anyone who found themselves lost. The pathetic-looking tent was dull in color, probably because it stood against thousands of storms within its lifetime. With each raindrop, its once-brilliant red and white stripes began to fade. It was as if the intruding rain was not water at all, maybe more like angry acid ready to strip any color that dares stand in its path! One white spotlight shone its dismal light on the main circus ring where there was once an act to see. Off to the side of the tent was one neon green stripe—the same shade as those strange brain spiders. Why would there be one green stripe in the middle of all the other red and white ones? My heart began to sink. I looked over at the sky, which said in red writing, *The Silence of a Circus.*

FLASH! FLASH! Suddenly, the bedroom filled with millions of tiny fireflies swarming like bullets all around me! Fireworks! They were like fireworks! Cutting through the dark room, the bugs glistened and twinkled, desperate to steal the beauty of starlight. I felt like I was put under a spell by renegade stars running wildly through the shadowed neighborhoods of galaxies. I lost my balance and fell to the ground where more and more fireflies began to fester! I never knew that these bugs could be so aggressive! I thought they were friendly! Crawling under the bed like a snake, I decided to take cover. The buzzing of the bugs grew louder and louder along with the pounding of my heart.

Just as I began to scream for help, the noise suddenly stopped. I slowly made my way out from under the bed and looked around. Not a single firefly was in my room. Everything looked unaffected. I had this overwhelming feeling that I needed to destroy *The Silence of a Circus*! As I rushed over to the windowsill to grab the comic book, the wind raised it in the air, let the comic linger for a little, and then carried it far away down the road. "Oh well," I figured. "Who needs any of that anyway?" As I watched the comic book fly in the night I couldn't help but notice the direction it was heading. I saw the comic blow down the street and over toward Center Avenue, where Wilde lives. I suddenly remembered the prank I had planned. It was time to let the night and my imagination lead the way!

The night was dark and muggy. The wild sounds of crickets shouted through the streets and made their way through the cracks of windows. How could anyone sleep like this? I wanted to be just as loud and powerful! Mostly, I wanted to rattle the nerves of that pesky little troll named Wilde. I made a plan.

I was going to pay Wilde a little visit at his house in the dead of night.

Wilde's house was so tall; it looked like it could reach the stars. There were deep, greenish-blue vines that grew against the siding. The vines went from the bottom of the house straight to the roof. Each window had dark purple shutters, one of which was permanently closed off by a chain-like vine. Like Wilde himself, this house had a strange vibe. Naturally, I wanted to take a peek inside! My plan to avoid getting caught was simple: I would enter the house from the broken basement window and tiptoe up the stairs into Wilde's room. I planned to hide under his bed and kick it to give him a good scare while filming the entire thing on my phone!

Once the clock struck midnight, I made my way over to the house. Why couldn't I just mind my own business? Maybe you can help me? You need to hear the rest.

CHAPTER FIVE

You

The strong, overwhelming feeling of regret swallowed my every thought as I was running towards Wilde's house. My brain was telling me to stop but my legs had other plans and kept going. Maybe I was still under the enchanting spell of the fireflies? Who am I kidding—I can't blame anyone but myself.

Chasing the moon and my own mischief, I started running from my grandparents' porch onto the cracked sidewalks that led to Center Avenue. Soon, however, my run turned into the tired walk of a zombie. I began to realize that Wilde's house was getting smaller and smaller even though I was getting closer. My eyes weren't the only ones playing a prank on me that night. Time got in on the fun, too! I had only been running for maybe five minutes but it felt like an eternity. I felt worn out and exhausted; but I turned around to see that my grandparents' house was not that far away. Did time stand still? I decided to give up and turn back. As I took my first step toward home, I heard an ear-splitting sound that almost knocked me off my feet.

The noise sounded like someone in the distance had stepped on a twig and it snapped against the roaring black silence of night. Could anyone else possibly be up this late at night? Horror Springs is filled with boring people who go to bed early! Just when I felt confident enough to start jogging again, I saw a strange, shadowy figure in the distance. The person or…thing I saw appeared to be walking along with such ease; it was as if they had no legs at all. Was this thing…floating? I squinted my eyes harder to get a better look.

The creature was wearing a huge black cloak with a long train that dragged behind it. The cloak's train looked like a thick endless carpet of pure mystery. It had to be at least twenty-five feet long! My eyes rested on the tiny flashes of little lights that were woven within each thread of the train. Maybe all of those wild fireflies found a home nestled on the tail of this cryptic cloak? Perhaps this anonymous Phantom was their leader? The cloaked figure didn't look back at me once, and I knew he was aware that I was there. As the Phantom floated along, his dazzling lights were both creepy and intriguing! I felt like I was watching the greatest show on earth. The hood of the cloak draped over the Phantom in such a haunting way! Is it possible to be so interested in something that you forget you are scared to death, too!? Being the loudmouth that I am, I finally yelled, "Hey, freak! Why are you wearing a cloak in the summer? Are you waiting for Horror Springs to see the next ice age or something? Do you live in an igloo?" Biggest mistake of my life. It was at that moment the mysterious figure raised something to his mouth and turned to me. Maybe it was a cup of tea?

So, yeah, I wasn't going to run in the Phantom's direction! I decided to head back to Wilde's house as fast as I could and stay clear of the caped crusader. The night was still young and I had enough time to pull the prank off before dawn. Running, running,

running, it was like I was a hamster on a wheel. I kept looking over at Wilde's house but it was as if it were getting further and further away! The night got darker, the moon got higher in the sky, and all I wanted was to get there, even though I knew it was a bad idea. Everything around me became frantic! Colors and shadows were jumping out at me! My own thoughts were eating me alive! Some strange paranoia filled the air. Oh, how I wish I had fallen over and broken my ankle and never made it to Wilde's house that night. I wish the yellow moonlight engulfed me and scared me straight enough to turn around! Maybe the moon could have grabbed me with its warm light and lifted me up? I would then be able to watch this show from above, rather than be the star standing center stage. Suddenly, time played its next trick. In an instant, I found myself standing on a rickety porch in front of a tall door covered in cracks and spider webs. At that moment, I felt like I had been in the deep spell of sleep for the entire run. Things were happening very fast. Too fast! I had… arrived.

Well, that right there was the last moment of my life. How many people can actually tell the story of their final moments in life? What does a dead man walking do once he realizes he doesn't have a lot of time left? He places his hand on the cobweb-infested doorknob of a hair-raising house and pushes the door open. The second my fingers wrapped around the doorknob, they became blue and white with frost. How could this be possible on a hot summer night? Well, apparently anything and everything is possible in Horror Springs.

CHAPTER SIX

Choose

My frozen fingers began to think again. There was no way I was going to walk through this door. I went with my original plan and started to make my way towards where the broken basement window was located. As I rounded to the back of the house under the watchful eye of the moon, I felt like I had gotten lost in another dimension.

I began to creep into the back of Wilde's

house. I never noticed this before, but on both sides of the house was a small, yet deep cornfield. In order to get to the backyard and broken basement window, I had to cross through the thick of the field. "Well," I figured, "There's no turning back now!" I took my first few steps into the tall, dry stalks. There is something really creepy about a cornfield after dark. Wherever my foot landed, the dry corn leaves would tear under my shoe creating a ferocious ripping sound that could wake up the dead. Suddenly, a dense fog rolled through and lingered above the corn stalks. It didn't matter which direction I turned, everything looked the same and every stalk was the same height. I felt like I was lost in the middle of a forest, yet I was simply in the middle of a small cornfield wedged next to Wilde's house. How lost could I be?

I remember my dad telling me once that if I looked up at the North Star, I could always find my way home. I desperately searched for it, but Horror Springs has a way of keeping you within its clutches. The great fog blocked any kind of starlight from coming through; it was even strong enough to extinguish the light of the moon. As I traveled deeper and deeper into the cornfield, the air got colder and colder. "Gosh, why is it so cold?" I managed to whisper through the shivers. As I muttered to myself, a huge cloud of vapor came out of my mouth as if I were a dragon living in the Arctic tundra. How could this be happening?!

Carrying my heavy chills and goose-bumps, I ran for my life as I felt my fingers and toes turn to ice. As my eyes watered, I waited for the tears to freeze on my face. Distracted by the thunder of my own pain, I didn't hear the warnings. Out of nowhere, I was knocked off my frozen feet by some sort of animal! I began to tumble endlessly down what felt like a hill. My body cartwheeled down frozen leaves that sliced me up and felt like little knives. The ground was slick like an ice-skating rink, so I couldn't get a grip and stop myself from plummeting through the unknown. Maybe falling wasn't such a bad thing considering the creature that knocked me over was probably waiting for me to stop!

The moment came. I stopped. Under the foggy moonlight, I could see a strange stone looming over me. It was flat and stood straight…almost like a…a…tombstone! There was a name on it. My frosted tears kept me from being able to read who the name was. I did see a date. It was the current year followed by a dash. The end date wasn't a date at all. In fact, it said the word FOREVER. Suddenly I saw red eyes gleaming into mine.

A thick black coat of fur covered everywhere my eyes could see. One heavy frozen paw was firmly standing on my chest while the other was gently placed on my neck. From what I could see, the claws of the beast were as long as rulers—and they were way too close to my face! As each claw slowly moved up and down my neck, the beast's foamy slobber rained all over me. His eyes looked me up and down like he was trying to figure me out. What was he waiting for? Why wasn't he eating me alive? In a moment of confidence, I decided to slap the beast's claw off my neck. He immediately jumped up on his hind legs and roared a heinous grumble of wrath. The beast's roar was so ferocious that the corn stalks around us bent over with fear. The fog also began to break apart and lift, leaving room for the moonlight to peak through and give me a better look at the monster.

From what I could see, the animal was magnificent. His slick, black coat had such a mirrored sheen that I could practically see my reflection. The beast's eyes were two deep, red laser beams that could probably pierce through just about anything. His claws were icy white and almost looked like they were made of glass. If I wasn't so afraid, I would have just stood there admiring his beauty. The beast's evil howl was interrupted by the echoes of an owl's haunting hoot coming from a tree in the distance, which caused him to quiver and whimper with intimidation and fear. It was clear he was afraid of the owl's howl! How could a huge monster like this possibly be afraid of a bird's distant chant? As the owl continued to sing, the beast gave me one last look. His red eyes locked onto mine as he stared at me for a brief moment. Then, the animal picked himself up and scurried deep into the darkness where my eyes could no longer detect him. Thanks to that owl, I am alive today. Well…sort of.

I got up, dusted myself off, and began to run before the beast could change his mind and come back to hunt me down. I have to say, it was pretty funny seeing such a colossal, violent beast so petrified at the sound of one bird's simple song. My whole life I wanted to be the hunter, but that night I realized being the whistling bird perched high above the treetops is way more powerful. The owl's simple song was enough to send the wild beast into a spiral of despair! That is the way of a warrior! I started to realize that a bird with a song is greater than a wicked- looking beast with no bite.

As I was running through the corn stalks, the moonlight led me to an opening in the brush. I chased the blank space until I found myself in a small open field at the back of Wilde's house. Finally! Despite the perils of the cornfield, I decided to still follow through with my planned prank. I had just escaped a huge beast; I figured there was nothing I couldn't do at this point!

Walking slowly and carefully, I rounded the side of the house to the broken basement window. I knelt down, took a deep breath, and gently pulled the window up. It was unlocked and very loose on its hinges. Even the slightest breeze could have blown this thing away. I slithered with ease and landed on my feet in Wilde's basement. I took a good look around. Everything was dusty and broken down. One thing I found kind of strange was how many different tent stakes there were in every corner of the basement. I figured Wilde's family must really like camping or something. In the far corner of the basement, I saw a wobbly old staircase that led to the upstairs. It was time to finish what I started.

Everything was going to plan…minus the whole running time warp, creepy Phantom, sudden ice age, attack of the mutant dog beast, and cornfield mayhem stuff. As I made my way up the stairs, every creak sent thunderbolts into my heart. When I reached the top step, a firefly whisked across my face and landed on my nose. I crossed both of my eyes to capture the light but then the bug flew madly around the room like it was trying to escape from something. I watched in wonderment as it erratically dashed down the hallway and landed on the doorknob of a bedroom. Like a moth to a flame, I went right over. Lucky for me, the door led to Wilde's room.

Standing in the middle of Wilde's room, I could see he was actually a lot like me. He had some of the same posters and games that I had back at home. He had the same exact blanket that I had. For a moment, I felt bad for him.

What I was about to do was not nice…but then again, I never said I was nice. I slid under his bed and waited. I felt like the owl perched on the treetops. I was about to sing my song. Or was I the beast with no bite?

While I was under Wilde's bed, I did sort of regret what I was doing. I turned on my side for a little and really thought about every-thing. Funny enough, right in front of my face under Wilde's bed was a copy of that strange comic book that ended up in my collection, *The Silence of a Circus*. I rested my fingers on the cover for a moment. I just needed to take a few breaths before I started kicking the bed. My pointer finger slipped inside and I started to gently open it. I felt a strange sense of calmness. I was in control yet I felt like I was tempting something. The paper was cold. The comic was in perfect condition, its pages glossy and smooth. *I'll just give the pages a little turn*, I thought. There I was, playing some sort of mind game against myself. Dare I open the comic book? The tension and suspense was killing me! I slid my fingers down the spine of the book and grabbed it with two hands now. I let my thumb open the first page—OUCH! A papercut? How could this happen right now?! I started to bleed. A lot. My blood felt cool like the pages of the comic.

Just then, Wilde started coughing violently. I nearly jumped out of my own skin. My body jerked from fear and I almost hit the top of his bed! I tried to take deep breaths to calm my racing heart as I began to slowly open the comic book again. Well, I wish I had opened it. It would have saved my life if I had read it in that moment.

In one moment of courage, you can change the world. In one moment of mischief, you can change your life. Sometimes we think that as long as we're brave, we can't do anything wrong…but that's not true. I was brave that day but I was wrong. I counted down…3…2…1.

I began to kick my feet up as hard as I could. *Boom*! *Boom*! *Boom*! With every hit I started to laugh louder and louder and louder until I couldn't even hear the sounds of my own kicks anymore. *This is amazing*, I thought! *Wow! Wilde must be so scared! I bet he's crying!* The echoes of my own mischief practically deafened me. In that moment, I felt like I was in a room of tin where every echo of my mischief was bouncing all around like an unseen ghost. I finally stopped kicking and started recording from my phone. "Wilde! Come out, come out wherever you are," I chanted! But I didn't hear a peep. What?! How could he not be freaked out? I slipped out from underneath the bed and stood up.

Surprise! Here I am! Guess what? No one was in the bed…so who was coughing? Where was Wilde? I just saw him…I thought? Suddenly, the bedroom lights flashed on. It was like I lived in a dark cave for years and one-million flashlights were pointed in my face at once. The lights exposed my little plan while blinding me! I was done for! Busted! It was Wilde's parents who caught me. But… they didn't really have a reaction.

Wilde's parents looked like they had cold blood running through their veins. They both appeared as if they had experienced every emotion one million times each and now they could no longer show any feelings at all. His dad was a tall guy who had very small, rat-like eyes. The whites of his eyes were slightly pink and his eyelashes were almost completely white. His lips had a permanent scowl and he stood with a curve in his back as if he couldn't stand tall any-more. Wilde's mother had long gray hair that was dull and split at the ends. She was sickly pale and her skin was almost trans-lucent, like paper. I saw every blue vein in her face, hands, and arms. Her veins looked like wild worms pointing in many differ-ent directions like a roadmap! Wilde's mom actually did stand pretty tall, but her eyes seemed more distant than Wilde's dad's. She seemed like she had lost her mind, found it, lost it again, and then bought a new one on discount!

"Hal, we were expecting you. What took you so long to get here?", his dad asked with-out any emotion.

Expected me? It was past midnight! How did his dad even know who I was? We never met! I looked over at his mom, who was glar-ing into my soul!

"Hal," she whispered, "It's late. Please stay over. Wilde will be excited to see you in the morning. He's on a camp trip right now."

I felt a shiver run down my back. There was no way Wilde was on a trip. I heard him coughing in bed! I saw him moving. Wilde's parents really freaked me out. In a storm of speed, I zipped past his parents and made my way down the stairs to the front door. They didn't react or turn in my direction. It was like they were stuck. Frozen. Or maybe they figured I would be back again soon?

That night, I ran faster than I ever have in my life. All the way home, I was crying. I didn't know what was going to happen to me in the morning. Were they going to tell my grand-parents? Are they a bunch of freaks that will come to my room tomorrow night? Why were they so calm? How could they not show any emotion at all?! I mean, I just broke into their home! I didn't sleep that night. Not a wink. I also never saw the entire family, including Wilde, ever again. However, there was one thing left: the house on Center Avenue covered in vines.

The next morning, I felt like I was stuck in a dream. I was waiting for a knock at the door. Where were they and why are they not anxious to tell my grandparents all about my little home invasion? They never did come by that day. Now I know that's because they never even existed. Sort of like me now, I guess. Please, don't leave me now! If you're tired, maybe you can try to read a few more pages? I'm just so lonely here. I can let you go, but please come back here to see me tomorrow night...same time...same place. Please!

CHAPTER SEVEN

Send

Have you ever told someone a story that was true and they didn't believe you? Maybe the desperation you felt to be taken seriously made you cry while telling the story? Have you ever been accused of "crying wolf," meaning you fibbed a little too much about things in the past and now nobody believes anything that comes out of your mouth? Maybe I have cried wolf one too many times in my life, but I needed people to hear me out on this. I had to go to my grandparents and do what no kid has ever wanted to do before…I told on myself. I came clean about what happened on Center Avenue that night at Wilde's house. I had to! I waited for the right moment when my grandparents seemed to be in an okay mood.

It was another dreary morning in Horror Springs. The air was humid and every room in the house was sticky. My grandparents wanted to eat breakfast outside on the porch and take advantage of the fact that it wasn't raining for once. As we sat down to pancakes, fruit, and eggs, I looked over toward Center Avenue. I couldn't see much but I did notice something a bit odd. It looked like Center Avenue was the only spot where there were no clouds, fog, or gloomy skies. I looked up and saw dark puffy clouds moving through the sky like salmon swimming. But the salmon clouds wouldn't dare swim above Wilde's house. The sky began to cry with a drizzle, but not over Wilde's block. The sun was shining over there with zero chance of rain! I felt like the sky was mocking me!

"Grandma. Grandpa," I whispered. "I need to come clean about something." They braced themselves.

"Well, the other night I wanted to pull a prank on Wilde, the boy who lives over on Center. I was running to his house after dark and something happened with the time zone! I was running and running but I wasn't getting anywhere and then suddenly, some freak sipping tea in a cloak came out of nowhere! So I ran and ran and ran and found myself freezing in a cornfield where I was attacked by a creature that hasn't been discovered by man yet. I think there was a tombstone with my name on it…but I'm clearly not dead yet!

Luckily, an owl saved my life; so I went into Wilde's basement and up the stairs where a firefly showed me Wilde's room. That was quite a polite gesture! Then I pranked Wilde, but he wasn't there and his creepy parents invited me to stay over, so I ran back home," I said with zero confidence. "I promise I won't ever do it again," I sheepishly added with hesitation.

There was a long period of silence. My grandparents looked like they were searching for the right words. Their eyes were darting back and forth. Their eyes looked like those slot machines in Vegas that in order to win big you need to match the pictures across. Slot machine eyes are the worst set of eyes because usually they come with the unexpected. Then came a reaction I didn't expect! Both my grandpa and grandma erupted in loud bellows of hysterical laughter. In fact, I could have sworn their laughter cleared the fog just like the beast's howl had!

"Oh! Wow, Hal! That is certainly something! This imagination you have is a gift! Where did you come up with such a great story? That house on Center has been abandoned for years and years! You must become an author or something! Bravo," my grandma chuckled.

Abandoned? Impossible! No way! I know what I know and I saw what I saw! It was clear I was on my own here. I needed to find my own answers. I looked out my window to the house on Center Avenue. The house was mocking and taunting me now. How could it be in the sunshine while I fester in the rain? New plan: I was going to pay it a little visit again tonight. I had nothing to lose and tons of answers to gain!

I don't think I have ever wished the daylight away more in my entire life. I wanted to pitch black cloak of night to come quickly. I waited for the stroke of midnight when I knew my grandparents would be asleep. This time I wasn't chasing the moon, I was capturing it. Instead of running to Wilde's house, I decided to walk. Despite my slow pace, I was standing on his porch in no time. Now, instead of breaking in, I decided to simply walk through the front door. To my surprise, the door opened with ease. Was someone expecting me? "It's showtime," I whispered to myself. Little did I know that "showtime" would be something that would end up destroying me...

I decided that going upstairs to Wilde's room would be a great place to start the show. With every step, my legs got heavier and heavier. At the top of the steps, the air was thin like it is on the top of a mountain. A little stream of moonlight was peeking through the cracked door of Wilde's bedroom inviting me in. I felt like someone was in there. I slowly opened the door to Wilde's bedroom. Everything appeared ordinary.

I know my grandparents told me that nobody has lived in that house for years and years. I get it…but you have to believe me! The room was perfect! No dust. No spider webs. Nothing! Every single thing was in place. It looked like Wilde had been living there for years. I got lost in my thoughts for a moment until the bedroom door suddenly slammed behind me. I leapt over to the handle to make sure I wasn't locked inside. Luckily, Wilde's door didn't have a lock. I figured it must have been the wind from the open window in front of me. I fell deeper into my thoughts as I tried to figure out exactly what I was going to do. Then it hit me. The comic book! I crouched down and grabbed it from underneath the bed. As I stood up, I was relieved to see the door was still open. But wait, wouldn't the wind blow the door open rather than closed since the window was across from the door? It seemed like someone or something wanted me to stay inside that room, but they certainly weren't forcing me to. I clutched the comic book close to my chest and ran for my life.

Heading back through the moonlight felt like I was in some kind of adventure book where I was the main character escaping from a crazy mission. In a way, all of this felt pretty awesome. I grabbed the comic book and got out alive…but it was just some lame comic book. I was proud of myself, but I didn't really know why. Still, I felt like I had won something. Now I realize that was not true at all. I had actually lost everything.

I continued to run towards home when I was suddenly stopped dead in my tracks like

I was under a trance. I got this overwhelming feeling that I needed to stop and read the comic book immediately. Suddenly, I felt like all I needed to know was in its pages.

My heart was racing and my hands were sweating. I didn't think it would be possible to open the comic with my hands sticking to the outside cover, which glistened under the streetlight. It had such a glow to it, like the inside pages were shining through. I took the deepest breath possible and slowly opened to the first page. Suddenly, a freezing wind blew the comic open in a way that gave every single page a moment to flash before my very eyes! The wind was strong enough to turn the pages, but smart enough to do it in a way where I saw every single page in an instant. My new story had just begun. Goodbye, Hal. Goodbye.

CHAPTER EIGHT

Help

As I breathed in the thick dust from the circus floor and listened to the distressing sounds of circus music, the feeling felt strangely familiar. Did I belong here? Was I the new dancing clown?

My mind began to race with storms of questions striking my curiosity like ferocious lightning bolts. Why? How? When? You name it, I asked it!

"Am I in a nightmare?" I asked myself.

The sights around me were blinding. The surrounding scents were suffocating. Music boomed with sharp echoes and pitch that bellowed deep within my stomach. Time stood still and so did I. I have to admit, there was something beautifully bizarre and peaceful about the stillness. I don't necessarily feel the same way now.

In that moment, I realized it's quite possible to get lost within the pages of a book you didn't write. It's easy to drown in the turning pages of someone's story, but sometimes you have to ask yourself how you got there.

As I've already admitted, it's hard for me avoid the temptations of mischief. To be honest, sometimes I would do something for attention to show off. Like the time I released mice from the school's science lab and put one in my teacher's purse! Or the time I filled a salt shaker with sugar at lunch, giving my friend

Matthew a whole new understanding of the name "sweet" potato fries. Yeah, I've made a mistake or two…or three…or four thousand, but did I deserve to be the star of my very own freak show? No! I don't think so! Yet there I was. There was just one thing left to do: figure this place out before I have to face the haunting glares of an audience.

I took a good look around. There was no doubt I was at a circus. My thoughts began to sort through my head brick by brick. I was convinced the comic book, Wilde the creep, the house on Center, and all the other freaky stuff that happened was all related. It had to be! I mean, even the title *The Silence of a Circus* was becoming my new world. Speaking of bricks, in an instant I felt like a whole bunch had fallen on me. I began to panic. Time to RUN FOR MY LIFE…if I still even have one.

Over in the distance, I saw a dark, shadowy tear in the tent. There didn't seem to be any sort of exit, so if I had to choose one way out, I was looking right at it. I ran straight ahead as fast as I could. As soon as I gained some momentum the floor swallowed me whole and I sank into the vicious quicksand I told you about. After escaping its jaws, I staggered over to the rip of freedom. Little did I know, this crazy circus tale had just begun.

Don't leave me now! I still need to tell you about the three doors that ended my life! As someone who always looked for trouble, I sure found it outside the tent that night. Wilde was right all along; trouble had already found me and wasn't letting go unless I picked the right door.

CHAPTER NINE

Please

Staring at the rip in the tent felt like I was standing on the edge of a cliff on a windy, dark, moonless night. What's beyond the shadows? Will I survive it? I threw my hands on either side of the tear with the force of angry elephants stampeding through the brush and trees of a wild forest. I secured my fingers on the tent and slowly pulled the hole further apart, which immediately reminded me of being under Wilde's bed and open-ing up the comic book the same way. I went slowly now, the sounds of tent stitches ripping and shredding soothed my paranoia of being trapped forever. Every stitch pulled was the tiny cry of freedom! "Just a bit more and I'm FREE—*OUCH*!" I cried. Suddenly, I felt a bunch of teeny nails drilling the bones of my fingers! Then came the cool touch of my own blood chilling down my arm, just like what happened under Wilde's bed.

I had no time for some annoying paper-cut...or tent cut. The blood, mystery in the air, and my frustration gave me the strength to rip through the entire side panel of the tent. As I looked up, the sky was covered by the red and white stripes of the heavy falling tent as it buried me alive. The tent weighed a ton, and then I felt my body drop into what seemed like more spider-infested quicksand!

My body tingled as I sank. I gained a sense of peace. I was as light as air! Was I on the horizon of a whole new dimension? Would I see new sights and colors never known to man? Could I have found myself thrust into a zero-gravity zone? Those few seconds of floating, they were all mine! I owned them. Nothing could take away that peace. Nobody could hurt me. I was safe for a handful of seconds. And somehow that felt like everything I needed. Maybe I was getting ahead of myself? In an instant I started gaining steady speed! Why am I falling now?! I had to brace for impact! I felt the ground getting closer and closer, ready to shatter my bones like glass. The floor below stole my peace and made sure its presence was known by teasing my imagination and paranoia! I closed my eyes so hard I thought they would slide to the back of my brain. Then, the strangest thing happened.

There was no *THUD*, *CRASH*, *SPLAT*, or *SLAM*. I floated. I hovered over the ground by just a couple of inches. Did a ghost catch me? Did I get caught in some sort of Phantom net before I could hit the ground? My mom always told me if you bite your tongue for too long, eventually you'll no longer be able to speak. So, I decided to scream. Clearly, I had become the new brunt of someone's sick little prank!

"Hey!" I yelled, hoping this prankster could hear me. "Whoever you are! Come out and show yourself! What kind of sick circus is this anyway? Show yourself right now! What are you so afraid of?"

In a flash, my body finished the fall and slammed on the ground. The fall caused me to take a big bite of dusty sand and dirt! I began to spit and wipe my mouth furiously just in case there were dusty radioactive spiders in there. I didn't come all this way for the spiders to crawl into my brain and make me into a creepy spider zombie! A flash of lightning suddenly overtook me. The bright, silent light wrapped up my five senses. Then came the great growl of thunder! I had no power. My opinion didn't matter. My existence was silent as a mouse. I was lost in the light!

POP! What was that noise? *POP! POP!* I heard an eerie stream of white noise like an old television on a dead channel. I looked up and realized I was under a dome, but this time it acted as one gigantic TV screen. A bright white light filled the dome and I felt like it could slice my eyes in half. Once the white faded, the screen started to play clips of when I met Wilde that summer day at Horror Springs! The scene then cut to me running to Wilde's house on Center Avenue and hiding under his bed. I was watching my whole experience at Horror Springs play out as if it was a movie and I was the star—but this was the type of movie you didn't want to be in; the type of movie you'd puke up your popcorn watching! I couldn't believe what was happening before my very eyes! As I was standing there, I felt chills crawl up and down my spine. The most chilling stuff was yet to come!

Imagine if there was a camera recording you every second of your day. Would you be okay with an audience watching it? Would you be proud? Watching my behavior on the big screen was kind of humiliating. It was clear I wasn't very nice to Wilde, or in general. As I stood there, I thought about how much of a loser I was. Why was it so important for me to perform? Why did I have to feel like I had more power than anyone all the time? There I was, watching my own imperfections, realizing I could very well be the last person on earth. I was left all alone with my chills and shame. I wished for every goosebump on my body that I had at least one friend, or maybe just one opportunity to right my wrongs. Suddenly, the screens went off and the sounds of the circus paraded through my inner thoughts and questions. I put my hands over my ears and knelt down. I so badly wanted to scream but I knew there was no use!

All of a sudden, the room went silent for ten seconds that felt like ten hours. Everything was so still, including my own breath. I then heard a strange, slow creak as if a doorknob was turning with trepidation. It was a dreadful and haunting turn that I felt deep inside my soul, like someone was opening the door to everything that I was! Then followed the clamor of dusty, slow footsteps. I began to look around frantically. There! I saw a shadowy figure walking towards me.

From what I could see he…or it…looked like they came out of some doorway beyond the shadows. Is there an exit here after all? Is "it" going to stand in *my* way? In the distance I could see the dark silhouette of three doors. Was I looking at three doors to freedom? From what I could see, the three doors stood extremely tall, maybe around fifty feet high. They were covered in old veins and webs. GROSS! I didn't want to know what kind of filthy goblin would live beyond those doors. But I could bet that filthy creature knows the way out! One of the doors was bound to set me free! Nothing was going to stand in my way, not even a gross gargoyle.

I gained some confidence and stormed up to the secretive creature and his three possible exits like a charging bull. It was as if I gained back everything I lost since I arrived at Horror Springs. Once I made it, I realized it was the same figure I saw that night running to Wilde's house. The spine-chilling Phantom with the heavy black cloak stood right in front of me. He placed his icy hands and fingers over my mouth and said, "Choose your door wisely, or you'll forever be in the Silent Circus."

Getting up close to the Phantom was both an honor and a nightmare. My curiosity was finally satisfied but I can't un-see his grim, merciless, sinister grin. I was standing eye to eye with him but I still couldn't really see his face. All I saw were his deep, hollowed eyes and his cruel smile. The Phantom's eyes were electric neon and looked like they were as deep as the darkest ocean. It was like looking into millions of stories, places, and times. Has he seen everything? Does he know everything? Is he a book with no end? Is he an entire library of endless possibility? His smile was ghoulish and sarcastic. It was an unsmiling smile! Before I could really figure him out, the Phantom muttered, "Before you choose which door, allow me to introduce them to you." He handed me an old, ripped scroll that unraveled to my feet. The scroll dropped down and rolled beyond the shadows; it had no end. I read every word carefully...or as much as I could see:

Welcome to my doors of three
Only one of them will truly set you free
You're here for a reason
and clearly not blessed
For you've lived your life
and created a mess.

Door one is a prison where
you'll live all alone
Not a person to be found

and you can't even moan
In a cage you will sit forever more
And wonder what on earth
was this ever for?

Door number two is a world
you've created yourself
You will sit in eternity on a dusty,
old shelf
People will pass and laugh
as they stare at you still
The expressionless look on your face
gives a thrill
They can pick you up and
place you wherever they please
Laughing and smirking you'll
become quite a tease.

Door three is a place where
the pages don't stop
But your voice and identity
will surely be dropped
You'll live in a place where
questions will be your own friends
Living every day you'll wish
you have made your amends.

Your goosebumps and chills
will come wherever you go
The loneliness will grip you
and only will grow
Regret and sadness and even despair
Will fill your life which you'll never,
ever repair.

    I decided to raise my hand and bravely point
to the door that I wanted to walk through.

My hand was heavy. Was I becoming bionic? My arm jiggled with nerves! It felt like I had become heavy steel and just lifting my arm was impossible. What was I about to do? Slowly, I pointed my finger down. I began to raise my metal arm up and show the Phantom that the door I wanted to open was number—

CHAPTER TEN

Don't

The days are long,
but time stands still
You can run but can't hide
from all of the chills
Questions and questions
but no one to ask
Learning the hard way
is not such an easy task.

Be kind and do well for everyone around
Or else soon you'll see
that nobody surrounds
Walk through door one
or two or even door three?
There is no guarantee
which doors will set you free!

All the King's horseman
and all the King's men
Couldn't save someone
who was meant to be dead
Step right up, get set,
and gather around
Wait longer and you too
will soon surely drown.

An audience of many is what most need
They sell their soul to purchase

the fame and the greed
In a circus that is silent
an audience won't sit
You can scream, dance, laugh,
and even throw a fit.

Alone in the spotlight as you so wish
When truly you are a bowl
as only one fish
Round and round you will swim
as you go
Loneliness is something you
will forever know.

You can be wise,
and your words can cut like a blade
But don't complain as you lie
down in the bed
that you made

I am the Phantom and
I make all the decisions
You'd be amazed at my tact
and my cunning precision.

I'll take your story and
rewrite all the pages for me
Your narrative and voice
will never be free!
I am quite lovable, I swear,
I'm not a bad ghost
For forgiveness and peace
I do love the most.

For poor, young Hal I gave him a choice
I let him choose which door
and gave him a voice
In fact, I am so very fair indeed!

For I showed him the truth
behind my doors of three.

I'll let him tell you for a bit
in his own special way
But then I'd like this story
back to tell, if I may
Again, I am fair, loving, and polite
But I'd be lying if I told you
I didn't love a good fright!

MWAHAHA! Carry on.

I guess it doesn't matter which door I picked because I walked through all three of them regardless. The Phantom took me everywhere! I am sure he will snatch my narrative and tell you all about the doors himself! The funny thing is, all three were inside the comic book, and now I am. Whoever else reads the comic book will be, too, even if I don't ever meet or see them. I will always be in search of others because I can't be the only one here! I will go crazy! More than anything, I just wish someone could hear me scream! If you ever find yourself around a mysterious comic book... run! Also, if you ever find yourself in front of three doors and a Phantom...make sure you—

CHAPTER ELEVEN

Forget

Door One

I hate to be a bother
I hate to be a bug
But Hal's really boring
I hate to be so smug.

Let's bring you to my first door
It'll intrigue you quite a bit
You'll handle it much better
Hal threw a ghastly fit!

One comes here when they're rude
And can't say a thing that is nice
The cage in which they'll sit
Will always be filled with mice.

Door one is a cold place
surrounded with icy bars
You can scream if you'd like,
but your voice won't travel far
A tiled room with one light
is where you'll have to stay
With darkness that surrounds you,
you wouldn't want to stray.

That single candle lit
can only last so long
To keep it you'll have to
admit everything
you've ever done wrong

In a cage of your mistakes,
you'll have to get some sleep
Never knowing who's around or
who can come and creep.

The temperature is cold,
just like your attitude
Maybe you should think twice
before being so rude?
If you live life talking bad
and being quite nasty
The people that you once loved
will disappear quite fast-ly.

Nobody likes to be around
a person with a bite
Misery loves company;
I guess that saying is right!
This is a place for the snakes

who spit poison all around
Their venom leaves traces
so no one can surround.

Poor Wilde was a good kid
He was nicer than our Hal
The two boys could have talked
And called each other pal.

But Wilde wasn't innocent
He was a trouble stirrer too!
So when he found himself in the circus
He chose door number two.

Door Two

You'll find yourself living
behind door number two
If you live a life of lies
and know nothing is true

People stay here when
their tongue is a powerful blade
And their words offer nothing
but a swift, ugly tirade.

Others like this truly belong on a shelf
Where people can pass
and be their own self
Collecting dust and bugs
is what you will do
Wishing you can take back your words
and start over a-new.

You can't move your face
or speak at all
Minutes will pass and you'll
wish you could fall
Watch people live their lives
free as a bird

Knowing you're on a shelf
because of your words.

The worst thing you can be
is stuck on a shelf
Instead of using your mind
to spread all of the wealth
Since I'm a fair Phantom
I will give you a break!
But know that this involves
a great deal of fake.

Like Wilde and his family
who chose to be mean
I'm not one to add on
and I keep my hands clean!
Door number two is where
the family must live
For they've been unwelcoming

and selfish,
never offering to give.

That's why the night Hal
chose to stop by
Mom and dad wished he stayed
and gave it a try
As a Phantom, I can't be forgiving
all of the time
So even if Hal stayed
they still must pay for the crime!

Now, back to the break I always will give
Sometimes it takes me much longer
to truly forgive
On a shelf you will stay
for all of the day
but at night I will allow you
to come out and play.

A dollhouse you'll live in
all through the night
Try and make things feel normal
with all of your might
Shelf by day and dollhouse by night
As the Phantom,
I do think this price is quite right.

So that house with the vines
at the far end of Center
The one that Hal foolishly
dared to just enter
That was a dollhouse of sadness,
desperation, and despair
As the Phantom I truly believe
it was fair!

Door Three

Now door number three
is an interesting place
You'll definitely feel
you have a lot of space
Behind this door,
there's room to roam
But like the other doors,
you'll still be all alone.

Third door living is no treat
Not only because there is no one to meet
For if you do find yourself here
It is your own reflection
you'll need to fear.

Now, our Hal decided to choose
door number three

Because he thought this door
would set him free
Little did he know,
this is the worst to choose
Because it's yourself that you
truly begin to lose.

This door holds a maze that never ends
No matter how badly you wish
you can mend
You won't remember how you got here
or if it's a dream
Your life and soul you'll wish to redeem.

Door three holds the secret
to other dimensions
Add this to my list of most
interesting confessions!
When the clock stops dead

at a certain hour
The world stops too
with a terrifying power.

If the time is right
and the stars align
Those who are malicious,
it is now their time!
That fateful day that Horror Springs
Pulled Hal in and made him King.

King of his own loneliness
and bitter heart
Let's face it:
nobody said this kid was smart
The only place to put people like this
Is in the pages of fiction
where they won't be missed.

The dome of night will take you in
All because your heart is made of tin
One day in a bookstore a child will find
The Silent Circus and it will remind
That those who have a darkened heart
Must try to do well and make
their words smart.

Everyone makes mistakes
and you must always try
To avoid hate and making others cry
Or you'll just be another kid
lost in the pages of a book
Where brilliant people
won't give you a second look.

Alone on a bookshelf you'll soon be lost
Because your icy words
have left quite a frost!

Door number three is not a place to be
For those who live here
I will never set free.

No candle for you like door number one
No dollhouse for you to play in and run
What's behind the third door
is what you've created
Old news you'll become
and gradually faded.

I give no sympathy to those behind
door number three
For those are the clowns
that have been mean to me
But since I am not a bitter,
wicked, mean Phantom
I'll let Hal finish his story.
I won't hold him to ransom!

CHAPTER TWELVE

About

THUMP! THUMP! THUMP! That's all I heard for about a five minute eternity. The cries of my own heart racing brought me peace. Who would have thought? The crippling shrills of my nervousness was way better than the demonic shrieks of the circus song. Sure enough, the peace ended, and the tent filled with its sad song of sorrow. Insert miserable circus jingle here:

ABOUT

DOO DOO DOODOO DOO
DOO DOO DO DOOOOOOO DO ...

Slow. Loud. Steady. The music antagonized my ears. Please, ears! Please! Get used to this chilling chant! This will be my theme song forever.

As I walked around the circular tent of dust, I noticed there was a rotted wooden gate leading into what looked like an old horse stable. Curiosity got the best of me and I decided to walk over. The dust under my shoes squealed loudly. My footsteps were booming as if they were trying to tell me something. Maybe they were trying to change my path and spare me?

Once I made it to the fence, I rested my hands on top and leaned forward to see what was inside. All I saw was unending blackness. There was a striking draft around the stable of endless shadows. Suddenly, a boney hand gently placed itself on mine. Before I could look up at who it belonged to, I was pulled over the fence and thrust inside!

The rowdy circus music sang through the depths of the darkness. I fell to the ground, one spotlight went on, and what surrounded me answered every single question I had since the moment I arrived at Horror Springs.

The music stopped. The silence. Oh! Please! I remember begging for it to stop! When the flash of lights exposed my surroundings the music died a quick, painful death. The quiet was turning my ears inside out! I wanted to plead for it to stop, but I couldn't! My ears felt like a vacuum sucking up the silence which was crawling its way to my brain like the radioactive spiders! I also felt like a hand was wrapped around my throat…maybe the hand that yanked me there in the first place, but nothing was around my neck at all! Silence!

Silence? Was that the answer all along? Was I was doomed for a life in silence?

My eyes darted around. I saw a sign that read *"Welcome to the Freak show!* A freak show? Sounds about right! Of course I found myself thrust into a freak show! Well, it was time I found myself out of it. I was getting kind of sick of that whole *I gotta get out of here but how?* kind of vibe.

I decided to step right up and walk down the long entryway into the show. It was dark and I had to keep my hands in front of me in case I bumped into something…or someone! I was scurrying down the path to finally enter into this supposed freak show. I kept trucking. Eventually the hallway ended. In front of me was a bookshelf made of mirrors and one candle flickering. That one flame made it possible for me to see my whole reflection. I was reintroduced to my new self. Unrecognizable.

Something was missing in me. Everything! I had no color. I had no dimension. I had nothing left. It was like someone poked a hole at the bottom of my foot and everything that made me…*me* leaked out. I felt this powerful rage overtake me! I didn't want to look at my face anymore! I licked my thumb and index finger and leaned toward the flame wanting to squash it with my bare hands. I took one step closer and felt two icy hands push me into the mirrors! I caught myself but suddenly the shelf was rotating with me on top of it!

The bookshelf took me to what looked like the other side of the freak show. Everywhere in sight were these glowing balloons of bright neon colors! Everything looked so electric and vivid! It was incredible. The colors were hypnotizing and brilliant! There were so many balloons I couldn't even walk comfortably or see what was too far ahead of me! I decided to keep going. Every move I made created static electricity! Tiny lightning bolts of static shock followed every move. Each strand of hair on my head was standing up straight. These shocks felt different, though. They were stronger. I decided to get smart! Popping these balloons to clear my path would be a pleasure! I'll start with this red one!

I took the balloon in my clutches. It was time I turned into the beast I met in the cornfield! I squished my claws into the electric red balloon and watched it pop in slow motion. I saw every piece of red rubber shatter as if it were glass right in front of my eyes. The red shards fell to the ground and smashed into even tinier pieces creating a sound as if it were a wind chime singing! As the balloon burst a flash of light blinded my eyes. I was left with broken red glass at my feet and dark spots in my eyes from the light.

I learned quickly that popping these balloons was not the answer.

I felt like I was being held hostage as I made my way gently past the balloons. If I were to accidentally pop more than one of these I probably would not survive the impact! I kept my eyes forward and steady. Every step was tense. What is that? I saw rustling in the balloons! I began to panic! Was it the Phantom? The rustling got more intense! Show yourself already! I began to scream! Another huge flash of light overtook me. Whoever it was must have popped like seven bomb balloons! Once the light settled I rubbed my eyes to help them get back to normal. In a flash I got this strong, overwhelming feeling that if I didn't get out of there I would die. Before I could turn around I heard a loud whisper close to my ear like someone was standing an inch from my face. My ear began to wiggle as the strange voice

cunningly whispered, "3...2...1...RUN." I
began to flee when I was interrupted by a cliff
and one shaky looking tightrope. I couldn't
see what was on the other side or down below.
All I knew was I had to walk it, or I was done
for. The tightrope was thin and wiry. I didn't
trust it. There was no way it could hold my
weight…but what choice did I have?

*DOO DOO DOODOO DOO
DOO DOO DO DOOOOOOO DO …*

I sang the sad song inside my head. I figured
if my mind wasn't still, then my feet wouldn't
be either. Okay, Hal. One foot in front of the
other. Arms steady and out straight. Here we
go. One step. As I looked down into the black
depths of nothingness, I realized how scary
it is not to know where the bottom of something lies. Have you ever swum in a murky

ocean or lake? You never really know what is swimming beside or underneath you! Perhaps something is just watching you? As I looked down I saw my breath create a small cloud of vapor because of the cold. I wished it was smoke. I wished I was a dragon so I could fly through this entire canyon of crazy! Suddenly I began to cry. I watched as one of my tears leaped from my face and into the never-ending galaxies below.

My first shaky step came to the second slippery step, led to the third anxious step, led to a strange shadowy creature walking the rope right behind me! Every step the creep took shook the thin wire madly! A thought struck me like the red electric balloon popping. If I am trapped here in this crazy circus, well, technically I have nothing to lose! If someone wants me here, they'll keep me here! I looked down at the endless tunnel of nothing that quite possibly could have been everything. I lifted one foot off the wire and hopped right off. I took a leap of faith.

There were hundreds of cages with people inside, but they didn't seem like regular people. I mean, they looked like me and all… but each of them was missing something. I went up to one cage. I rested my hands on the icy metal bars that separated me and…whatever this kid was. His eyes were white, his skin was pale. It was like something drained him of color…sort of like the kids I saw that morning at Horror Springs. Sort of like how I looked in the mirror. He had no emotion and just kept staring forward as if he had no choice. I leaned in closer and allowed my cheek to rest on the cold bars for a moment. The boy still didn't move. Was he frozen in time? My eyes searched his face for any sign of life. And then I noticed…the boy didn't have a mouth! Suddenly, the kid grabbed my hands and pushed his face close to mine. The cage rattled as his grip crushed my fingers! He kept shaking my hands back and forth violently, but he didn't make a sound! I was done for.

"Let go of me!" I yelled. "Get off of me, you freak!"

In an instant, the boy dropped my hands. Robotically, he took two steps back from the bars and continued to stare into space. It was as if the word, "freak," stopped him dead in his tracks. I was in a panic. These freaks in cages were all around me, and probably ready to break free! I began to scurry like a rat trapped in a maze! As I ran, I took a look at another cage. This time it was a girl. She was colorless, emotionless, and staring blankly, too. The only difference was, she didn't have ears! FREAK! FREAK! FREAK! I cried!

Every kid behind the cage bars was missing something on their face, whether it was a nose, eyes, mouth, or ears. None of them could speak, even the ones with mouths! The freaks lived in silence behind the dull luster of metal bars. They didn't even have the luxury of the circus music to keep them company! I kept running. It was clear I was getting nowhere. The room was an endless circle and I never seemed to pass the same cage twice!

I had to stop. It was like I was attached to a leash that someone pulled swiftly. I couldn't go further. I reached a peculiar cage that had one green bar standing next to the metal ones. It was an empty cell. Nobody was behind it yet. I stopped to get my breath and stared at it for a little while. I noticed there was a piece of paper on the ground in the center of the cage. Once again, curiosity drew me in like I was a dog salivating over a slice of bacon. I just had to get that paper. Suddenly my invisible leash became longer and I was able to step inside

Walking into the cell, I heard every single grain of dust slosh under the rubber of my sneakers. Every aroma grew with each step I took, and the air became thicker from the unsettling of the dirt. I was strutting through magnificent clouds of smog. My gait was peaceful but I could tell the dust, the silence, and the impending music hated what I was doing. It was as if someone didn't want me to cross into that cell and read what was on that page. But I did anyway.

The page was tattered and discolored like it had been there forever. I picked it up, wiped it down, and held it close to my face to read the tiny script writing it had:

Read me, write me, turn me, skip me
This is a page from your own book

You've wasted it with unkindness
Let's take a closer look.

You've been rude to those around you
You never really cared
Now I am here to flip the script
For it's your turn to be scared.

You see the kids with no eyes
Or the ones with no mouths
Some don't have tongues to speak
Because their lives have gone south.

They wasted all the good stuff
One is capable of being
They've ignored the truth behind
That seeing is believing.

The kids have spoken mean words
Seen only the things they've wanted

Heard what they wanted to hear
Selfish and undaunted.

When you close yourself off
And wish to hurt people
I'll take away your venom
And make everything equal.

You shouldn't use your eyes
To search for the bad in others
You shouldn't use your mouth to destroy
The beautiful life of another.

One shouldn't sniff for trouble
And be a nosy kid
Or listen to temptation
Like you just foolishly did.

I lifted my eyes from the haunting, deadly
words I had just read. This time, I actually

felt the rest of the color drain out of my face all the way down to my toes. I lifted my hand up close to my face. *What have I done? What have I just read?* My fingers were gray. I took a deep breath, dropped the page, and closed my eyes. Where was the thumping, chaotic heartbeat I called my only friend? I couldn't hear it from the deafening questions flooding my brain. As my eyes remained closed, I heard the slow creaking of the cell door moving. This time, curiosity didn't force me to open my eyes, turn around, and see what was happening. I already knew. The cell door was closing behind me. I didn't need to watch. I was just grateful the creaking sound broke the dreadful, smothering silence.

Even though I had just learned the most important lesson of my life, I won't be able to use it considering my life is here, behind door number three now. Remember when I told you that I survived my own demise and lived to tell the story? This is what I meant. I have watched myself vanish!

I do have one secret that I kept from you. I hope you can forgive me. Please, let me explain! Our time together seems to be running out. I need to tell you about the fourth door!

Remember that night I sneaked into Wilde's house? Yeah, well…about that. I didn't tell you that I also took a little detour to a cemetery that night. Curiosity got the best of me, and I decided to hide out behind the tombstones to give someone a little scare while they were walking by. Mainly, I was waiting to scare the creepy dude in the thick black cloak! I was mad that he had startled me while I was on my mission! Even though he wasn't bothering me, the fact that he was just standing there sipping tea annoyed me! Little did I know, that was THE Phantom. The reason for all of this mess! Speaking of mess, of course I chose to mess with him that night. I didn't know I was a pawn on his chess board! I had no clue that Horror Springs was his kingdom!

There was something very odd about this cemetery: there were no names and dates on ANY of the tombstones. I thought that was creepy, but still chose to look for trouble! Little did I know that I was already trapped within this crazy circus? When I saw the Phantom walking by, I jumped out from behind one of the graves and started throwing rocks at him. What a sucker...or so I thought. The only sucker was me! The Phantom turned in my direction, took his teacup, and poured all of it on the ground in front of him. As he was staring at me, his eyes seemed to turn into red beams of light. The way he glared made me feel like he knew everything about me, just like how Wilde made me feel that day when I dropped my comic books. The Phantom didn't say a word. He simply turned around and walked home. I headed back to the sidewalk after the Phantom took, what I thought, was his walk of shame home. Right where he poured his tea was a smoldering section of melted sidewalk. It was like his tea caused some kind of volcanic eruption right in the middle of Horror Springs. There was a small, smoking puddle left. Just a tiny little sip nestled within a small hole in the sidewalk remained. I decided to take two fingers, dip them into the toxic tea, and take a little taste for myself.

I thought I won that night. I certainly didn't.

CHAPTER THIRTEEN

Me

Tick tock around the clock
Excuses one can bring
No silly defenses here are true
When you're in my Horror Springs.

You can say you didn't mean it
You can bring me some tea
But offend me only once
Then your life belongs to me.

I'll take Chapter Thirteen
That number is for me
I'll bring you to the circus
Only you I will set free!

Door one is for the wicked
Door two is for the hateful
Door three is for everyone else
Who is truly ungrateful.

Door four is a certain place
For me to go and hide
I'll tell you with my own words
I'll gladly sure confide.

Door four is one you shouldn't pick
Some people have chosen so
I believe they thought too quickly
But door four they sure will go.

They'll learn the truth within this door
I'll tell them all of it
I'll answer all the questions
But here they will forever sit.

See curiosity gets the best of us
If we don't mind and be still
Knocking on all of the wrong doors
Can easily get ourselves killed.

If you find yourself in front of
A door that has a four
Keep knocking if you must
But you'll be doomed forevermore.

Each day, my cage door swings open and
I take center stage. It's like I'm some robot
programmed to take position in the center
ring. The warm, white spotlight whips
on and I'll look to the rows and rows of

non-existent audience members. The light is so bright. There are times when I'll imagine the stacks filled with smiling people clapping and watching me with admiration. Sometimes, I find myself dancing or singing for them but my movements are no longer my own. I am just a puppet on strings at the mercy of a Phantom puppet-master. I've tried to run out of here many times but I am always stopped by some sort of electric force field that surrounds everything. It can zap you to dust. I fall asleep at night to the sound of its sizzle, reminding me that I am never going to get out of this hallowed circus. Sometimes I cough up those green radioactive spiders and watch them cross beyond the force field. I wish so badly I could come along with them. I envy them. I want to be part of their world. Yet, I feel as though they were once kids like me who tried to run past the invisible bars of the force field. Zapped into nothing but a toxic bug of evil.

Anyway, as it turns out, I am the biggest clown of them all. My whole life, I wanted to become popular. Now here I stand…center ring to the loneliest show on Earth. Who am I performing for? I've been acting my whole life for attention; but now that I am forced to perform, there is no one here to watch.

OH! Do you hear that? Probably not because you are safe and sound where you are. PROBABLY NOT because it's really nothing but silence anyway. My heartbeat, my footsteps, the chilling creaking of doorknobs, this awful circus chant…none of it existed. All of it is just for my ears to hear. The world will never hear a thing from me and my world. I'm probably millions and millions of light years away from you! Anyway,

I have to go now. The spotlight is on and the music is blaring. It's showtime for me. My puppet-master awaits! Please come back tomorrow and open this book. I'll have more to say. Just keep checking the pages! Don't leave me here performing forever. I am not here for the Phantom's twisted entertainment! Gosh, the music is so loud I can't even hear myself think anymore. Is there even a "myself," left?

I can't ———

There's someone ———

Gosh, I can't stop dancing! What is this? I know that "sound" anywhere. It is the deadly turning of a doorknob that leads to the unknown. Who is that? I don't believe I recognize them. I see one hand waving me in coming from door four. It is not the Phantom's chilling hand! Should I dare? Maybe after this dance …

Gather around if you dare
The show will soon begin
The main attraction is a boy
Who surely will not win.

He's not a lion that jumps through hoops
He's not a bearded lady
The boy is more peculiar
And certainly is more shady.

He's here for your entertainment
Throw some peanuts his way
The strangest thing about him?
He is here every day.

Have you ever met a boy
Who had no voice or self?
What's the difference between him
And a doll up on a shelf?

Come down to the most silent show
in this hallowed town
Take a glimpse at our very own
Silent and sad clown.

Join me for tea later
I'll spill some more your way
Just don't give me a scare that strong
or the circus will have you one day.

I am truly a Phantom
I live in a world that's absurd
But please remember one thing
It is I who will have the last word.

THE PHANTOM'S
TEA TABLE:

Behind the Tea!

DOOR NUMBER FOUR
(ALTERNATE ENDING)

Once I caught my breath, I decided to approach the shadowy figure coming out of the fourth door. I walked slowly, knowing that I might not survive what I was about to see. As I stepped forward, it was clear I was slipping into quicksand again. I didn't care this time! I just had to know what was beyond the fourth door, even if it made things worse.

By the time I got to the door, I was waist-deep in sand and spiders. To my surprise, no one was at the door. Was I seeing things? All I saw was the door cracked open ever so slightly. I rested my fingers within the crack and braced myself. There I was, once again, about to open something I was not supposed to touch. They say if you keep knocking on a door—or in my case, barging in—someone you don't want to meet is going to answer. I took a deep breath and swung the door open. A vicious gust of wind propelled me forward and I landed in what felt like a car seat. Suddenly, a spotlight went on and I could see I was sitting in an old, abandoned roller coaster car on a rickety track. I began to climb out when abruptly the roller coaster started to move. I put on the frayed seat belt and held on tight. I knew this was going to be a nightmarish ride. The terrorizing roar of circus music began to haunt my ears and soul barging in on my every waking thought. Kind of like how I stormed into door four. The tunes were so loud they could shatter glass and stop time dead in its tracks.

The roller coaster went slow at first, then reached lightning-fast speed. I began to scream and cry and beg for it to stop. I couldn't see anything in the pitch-black darkness, and I wasn't sure if the roller coaster was going to derail or run right off a cliff. I then heard the grimacing chant of a poem echo from beyond the darkness.

Door four is a wild ride you see
There are twists, bumps, and turns
Climb on board if you dare
And feel your stomach churn.

I'll start the ride off nice and slow
That'll give you a nice sigh
Then I'll flip the script real quickly
You'll think you are about to die.

A murderer I am not
I don't take any lives
I simply change all I meet
And maybe give some hives.

Who doesn't love a 'coaster
With dips, drops, and dives?
Who doesn't love a good scare
That makes us fear for our lives?

I'd never have a boring 'coaster
For those to sit and have fun
I'd rather add a twist
That'll make you want to run.

When Hal hit the peak
And waited for the drop
He took a breath and waited
But heard a big, strange POP!

Suddenly it was raining
Things he couldn't see
I decided to turn the lights on
I counted 1-2-3.

What Hal saw was chilling
It was something quite profound
For he started to realize quickly
I dropped snakes all around!

They were slithery and evil
Dug up from the deepest ground
With red eyes and sharp fangs
They were the most
venomous snakes I found.

They'll creep and crawl all over
Maybe take a bite or two
But forever they will crawl and climb
Simply all over you.

Door four is for those who don't learn
The lessons life can teach
No reason or rationality
Will these people ever reach.

A roller coaster can be fun
If you can see where it's going
But nobody or no one
Is truly all knowing.

Up and down you will go
There truly is no stopping
This 'coaster doesn't end
The snakes will keep on flopping
Your new friends they'll become
Soon you'll be hissing too
It will make you feel quite numb.

Your words were pointless anyway
You used them to cause pain

Snakes don't have ears you know?
So your own will not remain!

Enjoy the ride, kids!
It's free for those to ride!
Climb on if you dare!
This is what you'll decide!

Over time you will see a change
Your body will soon wither
Look! It's your final form!
You're now a snake that slithers.

A snake low to the ground
Can bite those who pass by
That's why you're on a 'coaster
So you'll never give it a try.

Alone in your own world
With snakes that are like you

Unable to bite others
And make them feel so blue.

Eventually on this ride
You'll change again once more
To something that is verminous
That's the sadness behind door four.

When we keep doing bad
And it's all we start to know
We change for the worse
Our lives we simply throw.

Eventually on the 'coaster
You'll begin to stew and squirm
But your final transformation
Will make you into a worm.

A snake has power
That's used to hurt and kill

But a worm is pathetic
And never ever will.

Worms and shadows are left
Behind our fourth door
I tried to warn our Hal
But he wanted to learn more.

This brings us to the last words
For those who are leaving
With lessons I sure leave you
I hope they are weaving.

Be careful what you look for
In this life that is your own
Keep searching for the wrong things
And you'll end up quite alone.

To be a snake or a worm or a person
With nothing nice to say

Is something I wouldn't want
Every single day.

I'm a Phantom who loves peace
I welcome the sunshine
Bring me clouds if you dare
And I'll make sure you're all mine.

Q&A WITH DANICA MENDEZ-LIAKOS

Q. What was your inspiration behind this particular book?

A. I had a lot of inspiration! I wanted the book to have a lot of hidden morals in it! Writing a horror story is a lot of fun but adding a lot of meaning to it was even better! I think the book teaches the audience about the importance of kindness, and how if you are not good to others your life can become silent, out of your control, and almost like a maze of misery! Once you are in a life like that, it's like being in too deep and anything you do makes things worse!

Q. What is your favorite quote from the book?

A. My favorite quote is, "My whole life I wanted to be the hunter, but that night I realized being the whistling bird perched high above the treetops is way more powerful. The owl's simple song was enough to send the wild beast into a spiral of despair! That is the way of a warrior! I started to realize that a bird with a song is greater than a wicked-looking beast with no bite."

What a lesson that is! People think birds are weak compared to vicious beasts but like the Phantom, I flipped that script! It takes more strength to stay true to yourself and kind than it does to act on anger and aggression. The bird represents strength and the beast represents weakness! I can't tell you how many times my own song has driven bullies insane! That's because I refuse to stop singing!

Q. Do you identify with any characters in the book?

A. Hal and I are opposites! I was never a bully! However, some of the quotes Hal says are me peeking through the narrative. The quote, "I started to realize that a bird with a song is greater than a wicked looking beast with no bite" is all Danica! I learned this lesson later in life, actually! I also hear a lot of myself within the Phantom! He is quite funny but can cut to the chase pretty quickly…just like me! It's so funny because the Phantom is the villain, but I think he's more likeable than Hal!

Q. What are some fun facts about the book?

A. I wrote half of it way up in the sky on a plane to California after a long day of teaching! Also, when I was re-reading the book I forgot the ending and started freaking out when Hal said he had a secret to confess! I filmed my reaction, actually! It was pretty funny! Oh! I forgot to mention! My computer crashed so many mysterious times during the writing process! In fact, it just crashed five minutes ago!

Q. What can we expect from you and the Phantom's Tea?

A. The best is yet to come for me and Phantom! We have a lot of stories to tell and lessons to teach! The next few stories are even scarier and more suspenseful! The Phantom has just begun with a new pot of tea brewing! We have a possessed dress, haunted mirror, and so much more coming to the tea table!

Q. Which door would you choose?

A. I think the less of the four evils is door number two because at least the Phantom gives you a break at night when your world becomes a dollhouse. But then again, I don't think I could deal with all that fake! Maybe I would just stay on that shelf!

WHAT WOULD YOU DO IF . . .

If the Phantom can flip the script, so can you! Write yourself into the Silent Circus with author Danica Mendez-Liakos…if you dare!

The light of the moon showed me the way, but I'm not quite sure I wanted to necessarily see what was around me in the first place. I found myself standing in front of three doors. I just knew there was trouble behind each of them. I had no choice. Freedom could be on the other side of at least one of them. My name is _____. The beginning of my end started the second I placed my hand on the doorknob of door number _____.

A violent gust of wind ripped door number _____ off the hinges the second I turned the knob! Once I got myself together I noticed that *the beast of the cornfield/the Phantom/Hal/Wilde* was standing right in front of me. "Hey," I muttered as an attempt to break the ice. "Is the way out of here through this door?" I sheepishly asked. Suddenly, *the beast of the cornfield/the Phantom/Hal/Wilde* grabbed my hand, and the flash of a white light nearly knocked us off our feet. The dome I was under started to project a message in the sky! It said:

_____ (your name) oh
_____ (your name)
I see you want a fright
What brings you here anyway?
on such a gloomy night?

Why cross through the doors of doom?
Why bring yourself here?
I guess I can assume
You truly have no fear?

To write yourself in this comic book
Of twists and turns so grim
Is not as smart as it seems
I'm assuming you're quite dim!

I'll let you choose a friend
To help you on your way
But you must never be apart
Through each and every day.

Be careful who you pick
You really can't trust any
Choose carefully my dear
Or it'll cost a pretty penny.

I decided to call out *the beast of the corn-field/the Phantom/Hal/Wilde* as my choice. I hoped I wouldn't regret that. Suddenly, my new-found confidant appeared and we were ready to find our way out of the Silent Circus! As we both began to walk, we noticed a bright green door in the distance! That was definitely the way out, I thought! We decided to spring toward the green mystery door but stopped dead in our tracks when we realized our door to freedom had a giant "5" on the front in red paint! Should we take the risk? Was this the way out? I walked right up to the door and rested my fingers on the knob. With one deep breath, my grip grew tighter. I took one last look around as if something would jump out and save me. Nothing happened. I dropped my eyes to the ground and took one more deep breath. I decided to …

Now is your turn to become the author! Go ahead! Tell me what's behind Door Number Five! Did you even walk through it at all? Will it be a door of doom or a door to freedom? Give me your best chills!

_____

_____

_____

_____

_____

_____

_____

_____

_____

_____